Lexi
the Firefly
Fairy

For Grace Massiue, with lots of love

Special thanks to Sue Mongredien

ISBN 978-0-545-27045-8

Previously published as Twilight Fairies #2: *Lexi the Firefly Fairy* by Orchard U.K. in 2010.

12 11 10 9 8 7 6 5   12 13 14 15/0

Printed in the U.S.A.   40

This edition first printing, July 2011

Lexi
the Firefly
Fairy

by Daisy Meadows

SCHOLASTIC INC.

New York   Toronto   London   Auckland
Sydney   Mexico City   New Delhi   Hong Kong

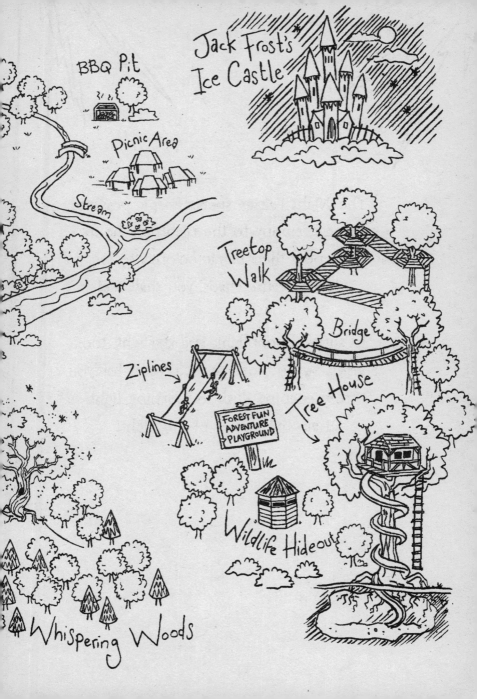

The Night Fairies' special magic powers
Bring harmony to the nighttime hours.
But now their magic belongs to me,
And I'll cause chaos, you shall see!

In sunset, moonlight, and starlight, too,
There'll be no more sweet dreams for you.
From evening dusk to morning light,
I am the master of the night!

Contents

A Face in the Bushes

The sun was setting and the evening
was growing cooler at Camp Stargaze.
Rachel Walker zipped up her fleece and
tucked an arm through Kirsty Tate's
to keep warm. Rachel and Kirsty were
best friends, and their families were on
vacation together for a week. Exciting

things always seemed to happen when the two girls got together. So far, this vacation was already looking like another very magical one!

Kirsty and Rachel were gathered with about twenty other kids at the edge of the campsite. There was going to be a special nighttime walk, and everyone was chatting happily as they waited for it to begin.

"Is everyone ready? Let's go into the Whispering Woods!" called Peter, one of the camp counselors. Kirsty and Rachel walked with the rest of the group into the forest. It was cool and dark underneath the leafy trees. Kirsty turned on her flashlight and pointed it ahead. The tall trees swayed in a gentle breeze, and their leaves really did seem to make a whispering sound. "It's creepy being here in the dark, isn't it?" she said to Rachel.

"Yeah, it is," Rachel replied, glancing around. "It makes you wonder what's hiding in those shadows."

"Whoooo-oooo-oooo!"

Rachel and Kirsty clutched at each other as they heard a ghostly wailing behind them. They spun around to see two boys, Lucas and Matt, laughing so hard they were doubled over. "Gotcha!" Matt cackled.

"Your faces! You looked terrified!" Lucas added, his eyes sparkling with mischief.

Kirsty and Rachel laughed, too, once their hearts had stopped racing. Then

Rachel had an idea, and she winked at Kirsty. "Oh, my goodness!" she said, pretending to gasp in fright. "Look up there — those two glowing eyes. They're staring down at us!" The boys gazed at

the tree where Rachel was pointing—
and now it was their turn to look scared.

"No way!" Matt yelped in alarm.
Shining out of the darkness
were two gleaming
lights that
looked exactly
like the eyes
of a wild
animal.
"What do you
think it is? A
mountain lion?"

"Hmmm," said Kirsty,
pretending to think. "It looks like
it's a really dangerous . . . *firefly*.
Actually, two fireflies!" She and Rachel
giggled. The glittering lights in the
tree were only a couple of flickering

fireflies—there was nothing scary or dangerous about them!

Peter, the leader, had overheard. "Wait until we get to the Twinkling Tree," he said. "It always has tons of fireflies around it. It's pretty high up, so you can see the lights of the fireflies from far away. It attracts other fireflies to it." He grinned. "When they're all

 twinkling on the branches, it looks like it's decorated for Christmas. Or like it's a tree that's full of fairy magic!"

Rachel and Kirsty smiled at one another. They knew all about fairy magic! They were friends with the

fairies, and often helped them—
especially if the horrible Jack Frost
and his sneaky goblins had been up
to their usual tricks!

The group started climbing a hill, but
Matt suddenly stopped walking. "What
was that? I just heard something," he
said, shining his flashlight into the dark
bushes.

Kirsty rolled her eyes at Rachel. "Matt,
are you trying to scare us again?" she
asked.

Matt shook his head. "No, honestly!

I heard a rustling
sound in the
bushes. Listen!"
The girls stopped
and listened. Matt
was right—there

was a rustling noise close by. "Are there bears out here?" Lucas wondered. He sounded nervous.

Peter smiled and shook his head. "No," he said. "It's probably just a badger. There's nothing to worry about."

Rachel, Kirsty, Lucas, and Matt all aimed their flashlights toward the bushes. Rachel hoped it was a badger—she'd never seen one before.

"There's a face!" Lucas cried out, pointing. He gulped. "I saw a face . . .

but it was green. What could that be?"

Matt started joking about aliens, but Peter remained calm. He explained that it was probably just animals moving around in the green leaves, and that it had only *looked* like a face. Still, Rachel and Kirsty exchanged a worried glance. They were pretty sure the green face didn't belong to an alien or an animal, but something much worse: one of Jack Frost's goblins!

The Twinkling Tree

"Are you thinking what I'm thinking?" Rachel asked Kirsty in a low voice.

Kirsty nodded. "Goblins!" she whispered. "There were goblins around yesterday when we helped Ava the Sunset Fairy, weren't there? There might be more tonight."

The day before, the girls had met the seven Night Fairies, who looked after the world between sunset and sunrise — but things were all wrong! The Night Fairies were having a party under the stars when Jack Frost and his goblins had stolen their magic bags of fairy dust! Since the fairies had lost their magic dust, strange things had been happening. Last night, a bright green sunset had filled the sky and the sun had not set until the girls helped Ava the Sunset Fairy.

"I wonder if we're going to have

another fairy adventure tonight," Rachel
whispered. Her arms
were prickly with
goose bumps. "I
hope so!"

"Me, too,"
Kirsty said
eagerly. "Let's
keep a lookout for
anything magical."

The group of campers continued slowly
up the hill. "I can't see any fireflies
now," Rachel realized, gazing at the
dark branches of the trees. "I wonder if
they're all at the Twinkling Tree."

"Probably," Kirsty said. "I can't wait
to see it."

After a few more minutes, Peter
stopped and spoke to the group. "We

should get our first glimpse of the Twinkling Tree soon," he said. He started walking again. "Once we climb up this last steep hill, you'll see it shining through the trees. Any minute . . . now! Oh." Disappointment filled his voice.

"That's strange," he said. "Where are they?" Rachel and Kirsty had reached the top of the hill, too. They could see a tall tree through the dusky sky, but its long, leafy branches were empty, without a single twinkle of firefly light to be seen.

Peter frowned. "That's a shame," he said. "Usually the Twinkling Tree is a real highlight of this walk. Where can all the fireflies be?"

Kirsty felt disappointed, but then Rachel nudged her. "Look," she whispered. "What's that?"

A small spark of light was dancing through the air toward them. Kirsty squinted to make out its shape in the darkness. Was it a firefly . . . or could it be a fairy? Somebody else had noticed the moving light, too. "Hey—look!" Matt called excitedly. "There's a firefly. Quick, steer it toward the Twinkling Tree so it can signal to its friends!"

The firefly—if it was a firefly—quickly swerved away as Lucas and Matt ran toward it. Rachel and Kirsty peered into the darkness, but the light vanished before they could really tell what it was.

Then Lucas gave a yell. "There are more over here!" he shouted, pointing at a cluster of sparkling lights that danced through the air in the distance.

The other kids rushed to see the sparkles. Kirsty was about to run after them, but Rachel put a hand on her arm. She had just noticed a tiny gleaming figure slip out of the shadows and fly toward them.

"Look!" Rachel whispered as she recognized the fairy's pretty, smiling face and wavy blond hair. The fairy had on a green headband, a silver sequined miniskirt, and matching high-top sneakers. It was Lexi the Firefly Fairy! "Hello again," Kirsty said in delight, holding her jacket pocket open wide so Lexi could dive into it and hide.

"Phew!" said Lexi. "That was close— I thought those boys had spotted me. I

made some flying sparkles to distract
them in the nick of time!"

Kirsty and
Rachel moved
out of sight,
behind the
low-hanging
branches
of the
Twinkling Tree.
"Good thinking," Rachel said with a
grin. "It's nice to see you again, Lexi.
We were wondering what had happened
to the fireflies that usually gather here.
Do you know?"

"I do," Lexi said. "It's all because of
Jack Frost. He knows how important
the fireflies are. Not only do they make
summer nights special in the human

world with their pretty flickering lights, but they also provide light to the Fairyland Palace and the fairies' toadstool houses. I usually have my magic bag of fire dust that keeps the fireflies nice and bright. But since Jack Frost and his goblins stole my dust, the fireflies' lights have gone out. Fairyland is in darkness!"

"Oh, no!" Kirsty said. "Can we help look for your bag of fire dust? We helped Ava find her sunbeam dust yesterday."

"I heard," Lexi said. "That's really good news! And, yes, I'd love you to help me,

too. Would you mind coming to
Fairyland with me?"

"Mind?" Rachel
echoed. "We'd
love to!" She
and Kirsty
knew that
they were
safe to
leave—the
other kids
wouldn't notice.

Time always stood still while the girls
were in Fairyland. They would be
able to fly off and have an exciting
adventure, and nobody in the human
world would realize they were gone!

"Fantastic," Lexi replied. "First, let me

turn you into fairies. . . ." She waved
her wand over the two girls. They felt
their bodies shrink smaller and smaller,
until they were the same size as Lexi.
Both girls had glittering fairy wings on
their backs, and they fluttered them in
delight!

"Now let's go to Fairyland!" Lexi cried, throwing more fairy dust over all three of them.

A sparkling whirlwind spun around, and Kirsty and Rachel were lifted up into the air. Another fairy adventure was beginning!

Fairyland in Darkness

Before long, Rachel and Kirsty felt themselves gently landing again. The glittering whirlwind cleared, and both girls blinked in surprise. Usually when they came to Fairyland, it was light and sunny there, with cute little toadstool houses, flowers everywhere, and the beautiful Fairyland Palace gleaming on the hillside.

Tonight, however, most of Fairyland was pitch black. It took a minute for the girls' and Lexi's eyes to adjust to the darkness.

"Wow," Rachel said, staring into the gloom. "Where are we? I can hardly see a thing!"

The end of Lexi's wand was sparkling, and she held it up in front of them like a flashlight. They could barely make out the vague outline of a toadstool house. "I think this is where Joy the Summer Vacation Fairy lives," Lexi replied. At that moment, the door of the house opened, and out came Joy herself.

"Lexi, is that you?" she asked, shivering. "Flicker's light won't go on."

"Where are you, Flicker?" Lexi called. "Are you there?"

From out of the darkness came the sound of beating wings, and then an insect flew over and landed on Lexi's palm. Neither Rachel nor Kirsty had ever seen a firefly close up before! They gazed in interest at Flicker's sleek black-and-gold shell.

Compared to the fairies, he was about the size that a robin would be in the human world, and his expression was sad.

"I usually sit on Joy's windowsill in the evenings to give her light," Flicker explained. "Once she's gone to bed, I fly to the stream with my friend

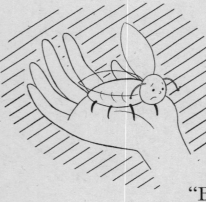

Glimmer. There's a night rose that grows there, and the nectar is delicious." His antennae drooped miserably. "But without my light, Glimmer won't be able to find me. And neither of us will be able to find the rose!"

"Oh, dear," Lexi said, stroking Flicker's back. "I'm sorry to hear that. We're searching for my magic bag of fire dust. As soon as we find it, I'll be able to turn all the fireflies' lights on again, but until then—"

Lexi stopped talking, her face alert. Kirsty and Rachel became aware of a commotion nearby and listened. They could hear voices—loud and angry—coming closer by the second.

"You're wrong!" the first voice grumbled. "I caught four, and you caught two. There's no use pretending you got the last one, because you didn't."

"Yes, I did! You're making things up!"

the second one shouted. "You're just jealous because I'm better at catching them than you!"

Kirsty and Rachel shrank into the shadows as the voices came even closer. The girls would know those loud, nasty voices anywhere—they belonged to the goblins!

"I wonder what they're up to," Joy whispered as they huddled in her doorway.

They didn't have to wait long to find out. The goblins suddenly came into view, and the four friends saw that they were carrying flashlights that cast golden beams through the darkness. They also held what looked like lanterns, but there was no light coming from them.

When the goblins spotted the fairies gathered outside Joy's house with Flicker on Lexi's palm, they looked delighted. "Look! There's another one!" the tallest goblin shouted. Then, before the fairies could stop him, he snatched Flicker, shoved him into a lantern, and ran off!

"Hey!" shouted Lexi, but it was too late. The goblins had vanished into the distance. The four fairies could now see other shadowy figures running around, all holding lanterns. From the goblins' shouts of glee, it was clear that they were stealing every single firefly they could find.

"Why are they taking the fireflies?" Rachel asked, bewildered.

"I don't know," Lexi said grimly, "but

32

I bet it has something to do with Jack Frost and my fire dust! I'm going to follow them. We have to find out what's going on."

"We'll come with you," Kirsty immediately offered.

"And I'll warn the other fairies what the goblins are up to," Joy declared.

"Thanks, Joy," said Lexi. Then she turned to Kirsty and Rachel. "Come on—there's no time to lose!"

Follow Those Goblins!

Kirsty, Rachel, and Lexi set off through the darkness. It was easy to follow the goblins because they were so noisy, and also because the goblins had flashlights to light their way. The three friends stayed back in the shadows so the goblins wouldn't spot them.

After a few minutes on the goblins' trail, Lexi's eyes narrowed. "They're going to Jack Frost's Ice Castle," she whispered. "I wonder what he's planning."

As they rounded a corner, the three fairies gasped in disbelief. Jack Frost's castle was usually a forbidding place with icy walls and stern guards, but this evening, it looked absolutely merry and welcoming. It was lit up like a firework against the dark sky. "Wow!" Kirsty sighed. "It looks so beautiful."

"Yes," Lexi said, sounding

angry. "It's only beautiful because he's used my special fire dust to light up all the fireflies he has trapped in the lanterns. Look!"

As Rachel and Kirsty flew across the moat and closer to the castle, they realized that Lexi was right. Glowing lanterns hung in every window, and inside each lantern a little firefly flickered. "How selfish!" Rachel insisted. "Stealing all the fireflies and trapping them, just so his castle can be bright!"

"I know," Lexi said. "The poor fireflies. They aren't as bright as usual—they must be feeling very sad."

"Look, there's Jack Frost," Kirsty whispered when she saw the spiky, cold figure appear in his doorway. "Hide!"

The three fairies hid inside a bush, and Lexi muttered some magic words that made the light of her wand go out.

They peeked through the leaves to see
Jack Frost holding a small bag that cast
a magical glow into the murky waters
of his moat. As the goblins marched
into the castle with their lanterns full of
fireflies, Jack Frost sprinkled fire dust on
each firefly, making it light up. "Now it
won't be dark
anymore," Jack
Frost said with
a smug smile
on his face.

"They caught so
many," Rachel said.
"I bet it was a goblin
that Lucas saw in the Whispering
Woods. Jack Frost must have sent the
goblins into the human world to steal
fireflies there, and in Fairyland, too!"

"We've got to rescue the fireflies," Lexi said. "We can't leave them trapped in lanterns as Jack Frost's prisoners. They should be free to fly around wherever they want!"

Kirsty and Rachel agreed. But how could they release the fireflies when they were right under Jack Frost's nose?

"We could sneak into the castle if it was dark," Kirsty said, "but we can't risk it now, not with the fireflies' lights flashing on and off. They'd see us immediately."

Rachel thought. "Is there a way to tell the fireflies to turn off their lights?" she wondered. "That would make everything dark again."

Lexi nodded. "I could use my wand to tell them," she replied, sounding more cheerful. "Let's see if it works."

She fluttered above the bushes and
muttered some
magic words. At
once, the tip
of her wand
sparkled in
the dark
sky. Then,
with another
magic command,
Lexi turned the
wand's light off.

Lexi, Kirsty, and Rachel held their
breath as they stared at the fireflies.
Had they seen Lexi's light? Had they
understood the message?

Some of the fireflies' lights vanished,
making the castle a little darker, but

most of the lanterns remained lit up.

"I'll try again," Lexi said, turning the light of her wand on again, and then off. This time, it seemed that more of the fireflies had seen her light and understood the message. Lots of their little lights turned to black, and the castle became much darker.

"It's working," Kirsty said excitedly. "Super smart fireflies!"

Lexi turned her wand on, then off, one more time. The last remaining fireflies turned their lights off, too — plunging Jack Frost's castle into total darkness.

"What's going on? Turn those lights back on!" the girls heard Jack Frost demand. Then they heard his footsteps hurrying into the castle. He was shouting frantically at the goblins.

"Now's our chance, come on!" Lexi whispered. She, Kirsty, and Rachel tiptoed toward the castle. Rachel held her breath as they crept silently up to the doorway.

Would Jack Frost see them? And what would he do if he did?

Glow, Glow, Glow!

Rachel, Kirsty, and Lexi pressed themselves against the walls as they snuck into Jack Frost's Ice Castle. They could hear his booming voice from inside the castle. He kept yelling for the lights to be turned on. Somehow, the three fairies made it down one of the hallways without anyone noticing them.

The three friends flew silently along the hall, struggling to see in the dark. They fluttered into every room they could find and opened  the lanterns, setting the fireflies free. "Quick, back to the fairy houses! You'll be safer there," Lexi whispered to the fireflies.

It was tricky, trying to work quickly in the darkness—and nerve-racking, too. All the while, they could hear Jack Frost yelling in the background. "What's wrong with this fire dust? Why did the fireflies stop shining? I don't want it to be dark!" he yelled.

"Hurry, hurry," Lexi encouraged Kirsty and Rachel. "We have to be as fast as we can!"

As the fireflies flew out of the castle windows, they turned their flickering lights back on. It was lovely to see them jet through the darkness like tiny shooting stars, twinkling in the night sky one after another.

On and on the fairies flew, from room to room, releasing the fireflies. The goblins had obviously told Jack Frost that the fireflies were escaping because the three friends heard him shout with rage. He ordered his goblins to chase after the fireflies and catch them again. "I will not put up with this darkness!" he thundered.

"He's so silly!" Lexi sighed. "The fireflies would happily light up his castle if he just asked them. Why did he have to try to trap them? They'll stay far away from him now."

"At least they can still glow from the magic dust Jack Frost sprinkled on them," Rachel pointed out. She opened another lantern and set free the firefly inside. "They can fly back to the toadstool houses now—and hopefully to the Twinkling Tree, too."

"Yes," Lexi agreed, "but the fire dust on them won't last forever." She opened

another lantern to let out the firefly, and
watched as it flew away. They were at
the very top of Jack Frost's castle now,
and the firefly soared into the air, its
light gleaming. "There," she said.
"That's the last
one. The fireflies
are all free!" She put
her hands on her
hips. "Now we just
need to get my bag
of fire dust away from
Jack Frost, and we can
get out of here."

Kirsty swallowed nervously. "How
are we going to do that?" she wondered
aloud. Sneaking into the Ice Castle and
setting the fireflies free had been scary
enough, but the thought of trying to get

Lexi's bag of fire dust from Jack Frost
was even scarier!

There was silence
while they all
thought. It was
hard to concentrate
when they could still
hear Jack Frost
shouting at his goblins.
"I need those fireflies back NOW!"
he bellowed.

His words gave Rachel an idea. "Jack
Frost really wants the fireflies . . . so
maybe we could trick him into thinking
we're fireflies," she suggested.

"Yes! If you could use your magic to
make us look like fireflies, Lexi, we'll be
able to get close to him—close enough

to grab the bag of fire dust!" Kirsty added.

"That's a great idea," Lexi said, waving her wand in a complicated pattern. Streams of bright magic spiraled from its end, swirling all around.

Seconds later, Kirsty and Rachel felt themselves shrinking smaller and smaller, until Lexi seemed like a giant next to them. "Now to make you glow, glow, glow!" Lexi smiled, waving her wand again.

Rachel giggled as she felt a fizzing sensation all over. When she looked

down, she could see that her legs and
feet were shining brightly. "Cool!" She
laughed.

The three of them flew through the
open window. Kirsty
and Rachel gleamed
just like two little
fireflies! They
swooped low
over the goblins
who were
gathered
outside with
Jack Frost.
Jack Frost saw
them and gave
a shout. "There
are two more! Catch them!"

Rachel and Kirsty zipped away in

different directions with goblins chasing after each of them. Rachel flew in big figure eights, while Kirsty flew in a zigzag pattern. The goblins puffed and panted trying to keep up. Soon Rachel was getting dizzy with all her figure eights, so she decided to zoom straight ahead with the goblins still chasing her. But Kirsty had had the same idea. She was also flying along in a straight line — headed straight for Rachel! "Watch out!" Lexi called in alarm. "You're going to crash!"

53

Firefly Magic

At the very last moment, Rachel swerved out of the way, and Kirsty zipped high in the air. But the goblins who'd been chasing them weren't as lucky. They ended up crashing into each other— and knocking over Jack Frost!

Just then, the moon slid out from
behind a cloud, casting a silvery light
over the grounds of the castle. Rachel
was excited to see that Jack Frost had
three or four goblins piled on top of him
and couldn't move. Even
better, she could see Lexi's
bag of fire dust sticking
out of his pocket!

She darted
down, her heart
thumping, and
managed to
pull out the
bag of dust.
She held it
tightly and flew
into the air.

It was

heavy! Luckily, Lexi had seen her. The fairy quickly waved her wand to make the bag light enough for Rachel to carry.

Then Lexi soared over to Rachel, and gratefully took the bag from her. "Nice work!" she exclaimed. "Come on, let's get out of here before the goblins untangle themselves!" The three friends flew over the moat and landed so

Lexi could turn Kirsty and Rachel back into fairies.

They were just about to take off again when Lexi noticed a group of fireflies, including Glimmer, on a thorny bush. Strange! Why hadn't they flown away with the others?

"Are you all right?" she asked the fireflies.

"We're fine," Glimmer replied, wiggling her antennae happily. "In fact, we're more than fine. We found a pretty

patch of night rose plants with plenty of delicious nectar, so we're going to make a new home here together."

"Oh, OK," Lexi replied. She smiled at Kirsty and Rachel. "At least Jack Frost and the goblins will have some light now. That's nice, I guess."

Once they were back in the Fairyland village, Lexi gathered all the fireflies that had come from the human world. She waved her wand and sent them back to the Whispering Woods, together with Kirsty and Rachel.

As the sparkly whirlwind vanished,

Kirsty and Rachel found that they were still fairy-size. They were fluttering at the top of the Twinkling Tree, along with hundreds of flickering fireflies!

"Wow!" cried the kids below. They gazed up at the tree that was now twinkling and sparkling all over, thanks to the fireflies' lights.

"They're back!" Peter shouted in delight. "There — doesn't it look amazing?"

Up in the tree, Lexi hugged Kirsty and Rachel good-bye. "Thanks for everything," she said. "Now I'd better turn you back to your usual size, so you

can see how pretty the tree looks from the ground, too!"

With the last wave of Lexi's wand, Kirsty and Rachel felt their bodies tingle with fairy magic. Seconds later, they were at the back of the group of campers, gazing up at the Twinkling Tree.

"Oh, wow." Rachel sighed. "It's beautiful!"

"The fireflies look like fairies," said a little girl nearby, and Rachel and Kirsty turned to smile at each other.

If only the girl knew that they had been fairies up there in the tree just seconds earlier!

"That was really exciting," Kirsty said happily. "Definitely the most de-*light*-ful adventure yet!"

RAINBOW magic
THE NIGHT FAIRIES

Rachel and Kirsty have helped Lexi,
but now it's time to help . . .

Zara
the Starlight Fairy!

Join their next nighttime adventure
in this magical sneak peek. . . .

A Star is Born!

"This telescope is huge, Kirsty!" Rachel Walker said to her best friend, Kirsty Tate. "I can't wait to look at the night sky."

"It's going to be amazing," Kirsty agreed as they stared up at the enormous silver telescope.

The girls were spending a week of summer vacation with their parents at Camp Stargaze, which had its very own observatory for studying the stars. The observatory was a square, white building with a large dome on top and charts and pictures of the night sky hanging on the walls. In the middle of the observatory stood the gigantic telescope. Professor Hetty, the camp astronomer, was explaining to Rachel, Kirsty, and the other kids about the stars and constellations.

"As you know, this area was chosen for Camp Stargaze because we can get really clear views of the night sky from here," Professor Hetty reminded them. She was a happy, round-faced woman with twinkling blue eyes and a mop of red hair. "Have any of you ever done a connect-the-dots picture?"

Everyone nodded.

"Well, a constellation is a lot like a connect-the-dots!" Professor Hetty explained with a smile. "A constellation is made of individual stars that you join together to make a picture, just like with connect-the-dots. Even though the stars look close together to us here on Earth, sometimes they're really millions of miles apart! Let's take a look, okay?"

Professor Hetty pressed a button on the wall. There was a noise overhead, and Rachel and Kirsty glanced up to see a large section of the domed roof slide back smoothly. This revealed the dark, velvety night sky. Sparkling silver stars twinkled here and there like diamonds in a jewelry box. Everyone gasped and clapped.

"Wonderful!" Professor Hetty said eagerly. "I never get tired of looking at the night sky. It's so magical."

Rachel nudged Kirsty. "Professor Hetty doesn't know just how magical the nighttime really is!" she whispered.

"I wonder if we'll meet another Night Fairy today," Kirsty murmured to Rachel as they all lined up to look through the telescope. "I'm so glad we found Ava's and Lexi's magic bags, but we still have five more to go!"

"Remember, we have to let the magic come to us," Rachel reminded her.

The girls' new friend, Alex, was first to use the telescope, and Professor Hetty showed her how to look through the eyepiece. Alex peered into the telescope eagerly.

"Everything looks so close!" She gasped.

"Can you see any pictures in the stars, Alex?" asked Professor Hetty.

"I think I see something. . . ." Alex leaned in closer to the telescope. "Oh!" She burst out laughing. "I can see a constellation shaped like a toothbrush!"

"Good job," said Professor Hetty. "And those of you who aren't using the telescope should be able to see it also if you look hard enough. . . ."

RAINBOW magic

These activities are magical!
Play dress-up, send friendship notes, and much more!

■ SCHOLASTIC
www.scholastic.com
www.rainbowmagiconline.com

HiT entertainment

RMACTIV

RAINBOW magic™

There's Magic in Every Series!

The Rainbow Fairies
The Weather Fairies
The Jewel Fairies
The Pet Fairies
The Fun Day Fairies
The Petal Fairies
The Dance Fairies
The Music Fairies
The Sports Fairies
The Party Fairies
The Ocean Fairies
The Night Fairies

Read them all!

www.scholastic.com
www.rainbowmagiconline.com

HIT entertainment

RMFAIRY4

RAINBOW magic™

SPECIAL EDITION

Three Books in Each One—
More Rainbow Magic Fun!

WITHDRAWN

For Every
Individual...

The
INDIANAPOLIS PUBLIC
Library

Renew by Phone
269-5222

Renew on the Web
www.imcpl.org

For General Library Information
please call 275-4100

www.rainbowmagiconline.com

RMSPECIAL6